Jessie Sima

be one of a kind. BE YOU.

For Thao, who helps
make my wishes come true

SIMON & SCHUSTER BOOKS FOR YOUNG READERS
An imprint of Simon & Schuster Children's Publishing Division
1230 Avenue of the Americas, New York, New York 10020
© 2022 by Jessie Sima
Book design by Lizzy Bromley © 2022 by Simon & Schuster, Inc.
All rights reserved, including the right of reproduction in whole or in part in any form.
SIMON & SCHUSTER BOOKS FOR YOUNG READERS and related marks are trademarks of Simon & Schuster, Inc.
For information about special discounts for bulk purchases, please contact Simon & Schuster
Special Sales at 1-866-506-1949 or business@simonandschuster.com.
The Simon & Schuster Speakers Bureau can bring authors to your live event. For more information
or to book an event, contact the Simon & Schuster Speakers Bureau at 1-866-248-3049 or
visit our website at www.simonspeakers.com.
The text for this book was set in ITC Lubalin Graph.
The illustrations for this book were rendered in Adobe Photoshop.
Manufactured in China · 1221 SCP · First Edition
2 4 6 8 10 9 7 5 3 1
Library of Congress Cataloging-in-Publication Data
Names: Sima, Jessie, author, illustrator.
Title: Perfectly pegasus / Jessie Sima.
Description: First edition. | New York : Simon & Schuster Books for Young Readers, [2022] | Audience: Ages 4-8. |
Audience: Grades K-1. | Summary: Nimbus, a lonely pegasus, searches for a fallen
star to wish for a friend and meets a unicorn named Kelp along the way.
Identifiers: LCCN 2021005324 (print) | LCCN 2021005325 (ebook) |
ISBN 9781534497177 (hardcover) | ISBN 9781534497184 (ebook)
Subjects: CYAC: Friendship—Fiction. | Pegasus (Greek mythology)—Fiction. |
Unicorns—Fiction. | Wishes—Fiction. | BISAC: JUVENILE FICTION / Animals / Dragons,
Unicorns & Mythical | JUVENILE FICTION / Social Themes / New Experience | LCGFT: Picture books.
Classification: LCC PZ7.1.S548 Pe 2022 (print) | LCC PZ7.1.S548 (ebook) | DDC [Fic]—dc23
LC record available at https://lccn.loc.gov/2021005324
LC ebook record available at https://lccn.loc.gov/2021005325

Perfectly PEGASUS

JESSIE SIMA

Simon & Schuster Books for Young Readers
New York   London   Toronto   Sydney   New Delhi

Nimbus was born high in the sky.

It was clear from the start she was one-of-a-kind.

She had wide, feathered wings,

she had a way with clouds,

and she had the whole sky to herself.

Usually that sky felt full of adventure.

But sometimes, it felt empty.

Whenever the sky started to feel *too* empty,
Nimbus traced pictures in the stars and dreamed
of having someone to keep her company.

It was on one of those nights . . .

that a perfect wishing star shot across the sky.

But it fell so quickly that Nimbus didn't
have time to make her wish.

I wish
I had
someone....

Far off in the distance she could make out the faint, warm glow of the star where it landed.

Nimbus flew toward the light as fast as she could,

which was very fast, indeed,

hoping she could locate the fallen star and finish her wish.

When she reached the ground, the sun was already high in the sky. It was too bright to see the star's shine.

Nimbus would just have to find the star without it. That didn't sound so hard.

It was.

Instead, she came face-to-face with a mysterious, sparkling creature . . .

named Kelp.

Kelp was impressed by Nimbus's wide, feathered wings.

Nimbus was amazed by Kelp's glittery horn.

So amazed that she nearly forgot why
she'd come to the island.

But then she remembered the empty sky,
and the wish she wanted to make.

Nimbus told Kelp all about her search for the fallen star.
To her surprise, he wanted to help.

Nimbus looked high.

Kelp looked low.

And together they explored most of the island.

But they did *not* find the star.

Nimbus had never heard of friends before.
They were all very pointy, and eager to help.

They searched here. . . .

They searched there. . . .

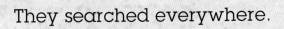

They searched everywhere.

But they did *not* find the star.
Nimbus was having fun on land,
but she felt discouraged.

If she couldn't find this star,
she would have to wait
for another to fall before
making her wish.

So Nimbus thanked Kelp and his pointy friends
for all their help, and returned to the sky.

We'll miss you!

Nimbus flew toward
the clouds a little
more slowly,

which was still
pretty fast, indeed,

resigning herself
to watch over the
night sky.

When she got there, the clouds were just as she'd left them.

But Nimbus felt different.

Now that she had met everyone on land,
her constellations were less of a consolation.

Would she ever see another falling star?

Would she ever get a chance
to wish for . . . friends?

Nimbus wasn't sure.

But then she realized that maybe . . .

just maybe . . .

her wish had already come true.

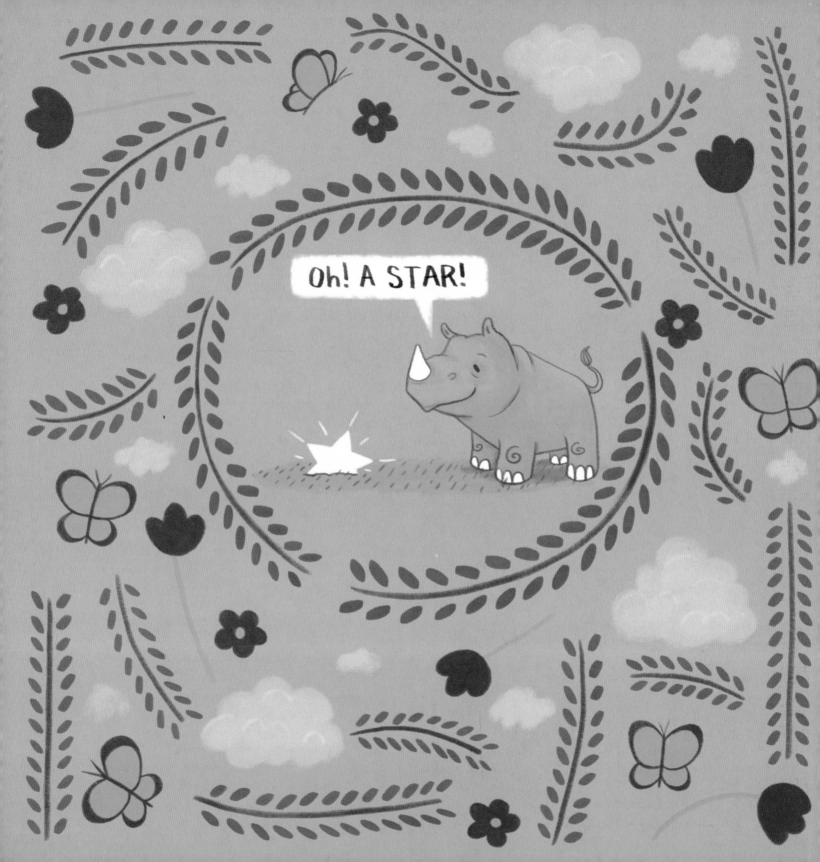